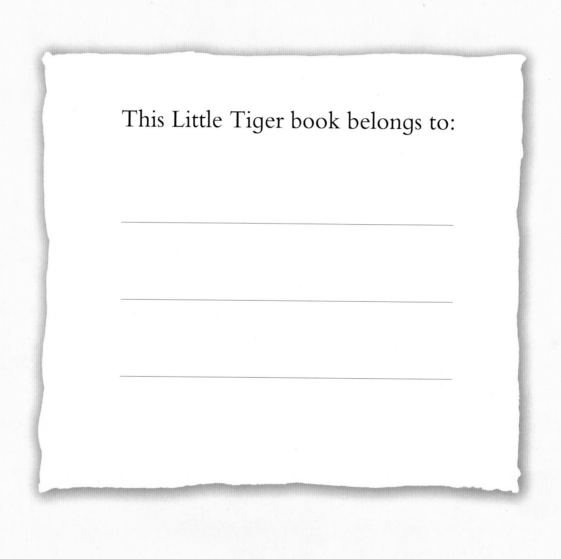

This Little Tiger book belongs to:

_____

_____

_____

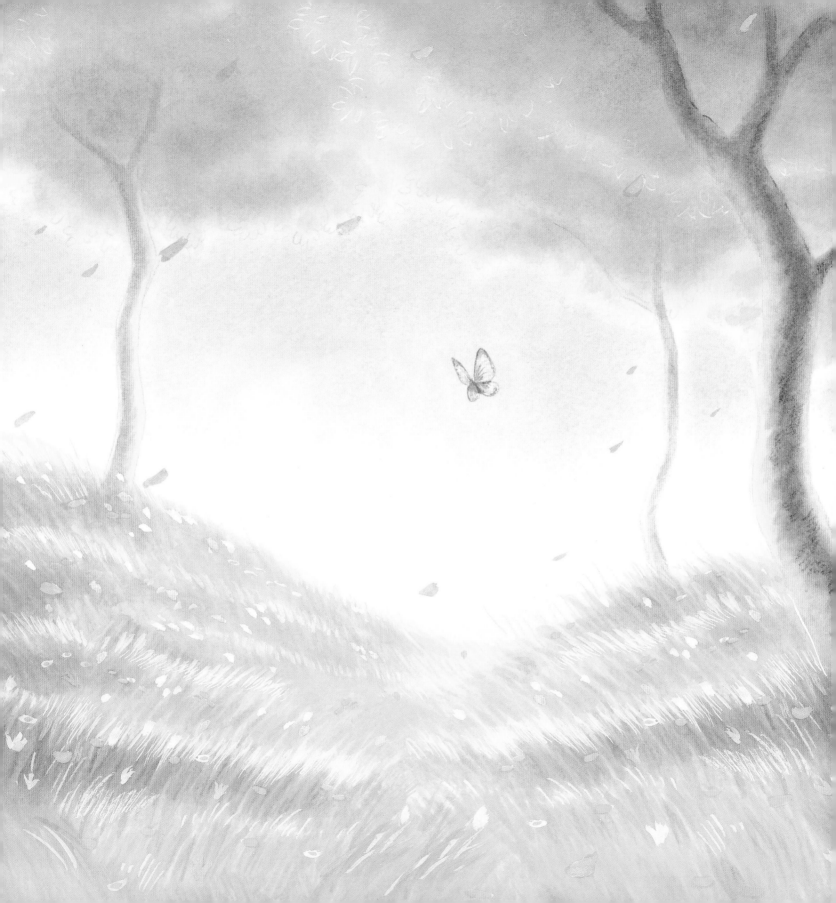

For Georgie, Bethany and Jemma ~ G L

Thanks to Mum, Dad, friends and myriad family. For Brianna, Isabelle, Gabrielle, Charlotte, Helena, Amy, Rachel, Tim and Ange ~ L H

LITTLE TIGER PRESS
1 The Coda Centre, 189 Munster Road, London SW6 6AW
www.littletiger.co.uk

First published in Great Britain 2006
This edition published 2016

Text copyright © Gill Lewis 2006
Illustrations copyright © Louise Ho 2006

Gill Lewis and Louise Ho have asserted their rights to be identified
as the author and illustrator of this work under the Copyright, Designs
and Patents Act, 1988

The Most Precious Thing

Gill Lewis

Louise Ho

LITTLE TIGER PRESS
London

Little Bear was taking Mummy Bear on a walk through the forest in the autumn sunlight. She wanted to show her the special place where the juiciest berries and the sweetest nuts could be found.

As Little Bear skipped through
the rustling leaves, she suddenly
spied a small blue stone glittering
in the sunshine.

"Look, Mummy, look!" cried Little Bear, picking
it up. "Look at this shiny jewel I have found."
Little Bear gazed as it sparkled in her paw.
"It must be the most precious thing in the whole
wide world," she gasped.

"Oh yes, Little Bear,
this is a very beautiful stone,"
said Mummy Bear, holding it
up so that it twinkled in the light,
"but the most precious thing is
even prettier than this."

"Really?" said Little Bear in wonder. She
put the stone carefully in her bag. "Let's go
and look! I want to find the most precious
thing EVER!"

"Wait for me," laughed Mummy Bear, as
Little Bear scampered off through the trees.

Little Bear and Mummy Bear played games in the afternoon sun. They tried to catch the seeds that spun in the breeze. And Little Bear kept looking for something prettier than the little blue stone.

After a while they came to Little Bear's special place and they filled their tummies with juicy purple blackberries.
Little Bear was reaching for a berry when she saw something pink hidden in the brambles . . .

It was a beautiful wild rose.
"Mummy!" shouted Little
Bear excitedly. "Come and
see what I have found!"

She stroked the rose's silky
petals and sniffed its sweet smell.
"I've never seen such a pretty
flower. Surely this must be the
most precious thing?"

"This rose is very pretty, Little Bear," said Mummy Bear, "and it's soft as velvet." She tickled the rose against Little Bear's nose, making her sneeze. "But the most precious thing is even softer than this."

Little Bear wondered what on earth could be softer
than her beautiful rose. She searched and searched
through the dry, crunchy leaves, but
she found only spiky horse chestnuts,
bristly pine cones and a
rather cross hedgehog!

Just then she caught sight of something fluttering high up
in the trees.

"Look up there!" she shouted. "That *has* to be it!"

Mummy Bear lifted Little Bear up
into the air. Caught in a spider's web
was a tiny fluffy feather. Little Bear
reached up high and took the feather
very gently in her paw.

Little Bear touched the downy
feather against her cheek.

"Oh Mummy," she whispered
hopefully. "Please tell me. Is this
the most precious thing?"

"It is very soft," said Mummy
Bear, "but the most precious thing
is even better than this – it makes
me want to dance for joy."

And Mummy Bear twirled Little
Bear round, making her giggle.

Little Bear was determined to find the most precious thing. She ran up a grassy hilltop to look out at the woods and fields. Hundreds of dazzling butterflies suddenly filled the air around her.

One of the butterflies landed lightly on her paw. Little Bear gazed at it in wonder.

"This is it!" she sang out happily. "At last I have found the most precious thing in the whole of the big wide world."

Little Bear and Mummy Bear lay in the long grass as the butterfly fluttered through the golden sunlight.

"Oh yes, that is very special," said Mummy Bear softly, "but I can hold the most precious thing safe and tight in my arms."

"Oh, please tell me what it is!" said Little Bear crossly. "I have looked absolutely everywhere and I still haven't found it."

Mummy Bear smiled. "The most precious thing is prettier than any jewel, is softer than a rose or the fluffiest feather, and fills me with more joy than a dancing butterfly. The most precious thing . . ." she said, hugging Little Bear tightly, ". . . is you!"

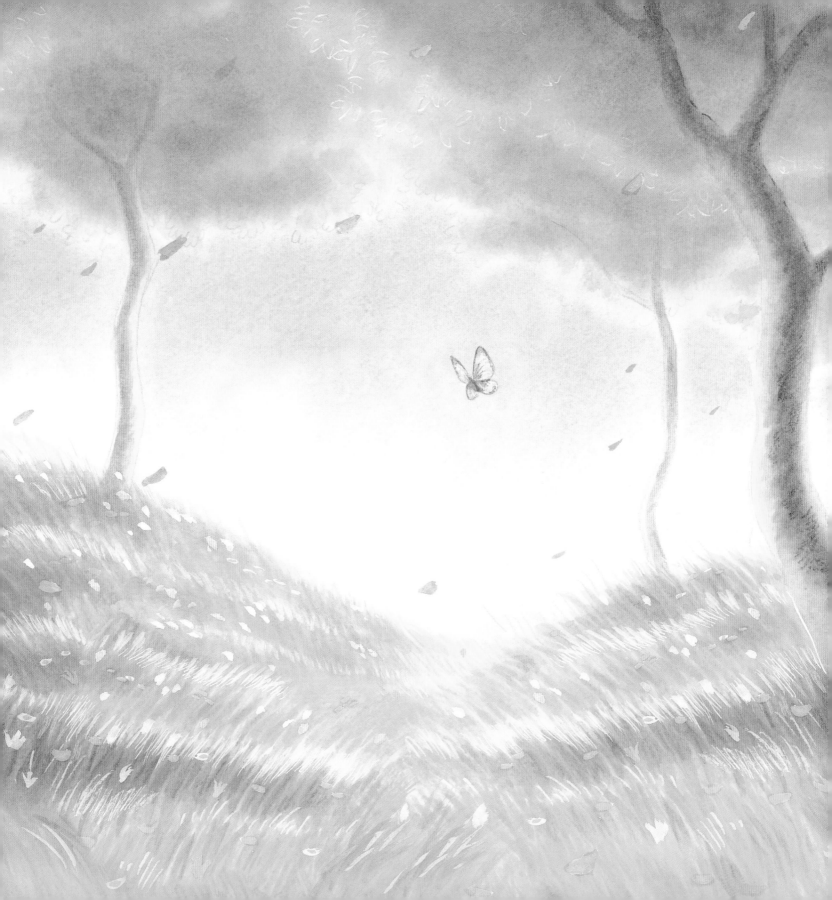